What Shall We Do When We All Go Out?

A Traditional Song, Illustrated by

Shari Halpern

North-South Books

New York / London

FOR JUDY SUE

Text adapted by Philip H. Bailey

Published in the United States by North-South Books Inc., New York.

*Published simultaneously in Great Britain, Canada, Australia, and
New Zealand in 1995 by North-South Books, an imprint of
Nord-Süd Verlag AG, Gossau Zürich, Switzerland.*

*Library of Congress Cataloging-in-Publication Data
What shall we do when we all go out? : a traditional song / illustrated
by Shari Halpern ; [text adapted by Philip H. Bailey].
Summary: Words and illustrations depict the activities
of the day as children go out to play.
1. Children's songs—Texts.   [1. Play—Songs and music. 2. Songs.]
I. Bailey, Philip H.   II. Title.
PZ8.3.H16Wh   1995
782.42'083—dc20
[E]   94-38573*

*A CIP catalogue record for this book is
available from The British Library.*

*ISBN 1-55858-424-2 (trade binding)
10 9 8 7 6 5 4 3 2 1
ISBN 1-55858-425-0 (library binding)
10 9 8 7 6 5 4 3 2 1*

*The artwork consists of collages made with
several different types of paper painted
with acrylics and watercolors, as well as
color photocopies of pieces of fabric.
Typography by Marc Cheshire.
The type is Laudatio.*

Printed in Belgium

**What shall we do when we all go out,
all go out, all go out?**

What shall we do when we all go out,
When we all go out to play?

We will ride our three-wheel bikes,
three-wheel bikes, three-wheel bikes.
We will ride our three-wheel bikes
When we all go out to play!

**We will seesaw up and down,
up and down, up and down.
We will seesaw up and down
When we all go out to play!**

We will run and somersault,
somersault, somersault.
We will run and somersault
When we all go out to play!

We will wear our roller skates,
roller skates, roller skates.
We will wear our roller skates
When we all go out to play!

Then we'll sit and eat our lunch,
eat our lunch, eat our lunch.
Then we'll sit and eat our lunch
In the middle of the day!

What shall we do in the afternoon,
afternoon, afternoon?
What shall we do in the afternoon
After we've had lunch?

We will stop to feed the ducks,
feed the ducks, feed the ducks.
We will stop to feed the ducks
After we've had lunch!

**We will fly our long-tailed kites,
long-tailed kites, long-tailed kites.
We will fly our long-tailed kites
After we've had lunch!**

We will climb a great big tree,
a great big tree, a great big tree.
We will climb a great big tree
When we all go back to play!

We will all play hide-and-seek,
hide-and-seek, hide-and-seek.
We will all play hide-and-seek
till it's time for us to go!

What shall we do when we all go in,
all go in, all go in?
What shall we do when we all go in,
When we all go in from play?

We will sit and sip our soup,
sip our soup, sip our soup.
We will sit and sip our soup
And think about TOMORROW!